FIRM BANKER DADDY

DADDY'S LITTLE GIRL SERIES

SCOTT WYLDER

CONTENTS

1

Tris

I STARED at the financial records in my hand. This couldn't be right. I know my mom got into a lot of trouble with her gambling addiction, but this was something else.

However, glaring back up at me, plain as day, was a note from a loan shark. For ten grand. Even though most of my mother's debts disappeared with her death, I knew this one wasn't going away.

I worked from home as a virtual assistant. I made enough to get by, but definitely, nothing that would cover this. "What did you do, mom?" I whispered.

I looked around my mom's tiny house. It was more of a cottage than a house, but without any of the charm. It was a cramped one-bedroom place that was filthy. Dirty clothes covered the stained carpet on her bedroom and dirty dishes were in the sink, slowly molding. Cobwebs hung like decorations in the hallways and dead bugs littered the ground.

But the living room was what really made me sick to my stomach. Boxes and boxes of brand new merchandise filled the room, practically smothering the ratty couch and TV stand. Mom was easily distracted by new shiny things, and that unfortunately included pyramid schemes disguised as business opportunities. Any money she actually earned went right into pyramid schemes and gambling.

She had left everything to me. And now I was the proud owner of the depressing remains of her life. But my own life might be in danger if I had to worry about a loan shark.

I had planned to start cleaning my mom's house that day but I ended up leaving without doing anything. It was already painful enough to be in there but now I had to worry about a loan shark.

I took a deep breath as I went to my apartment to take a shower. I needed to think about this rationally. There was no way I could afford that loan but I couldn't just let it fester.

As I got into the shower, I tried to think, but it was difficult. My head felt foggy. My mother had only passed away a week ago and it was already difficult enough just walking into her place.

There were too many bad memories. We had never been close. I suppose she tried her best as a mother, but it didn't change the fact that I had basically raised myself while she squandered away our money. When I was old enough to get a part-time job after school, I had to hide that money from her or she would steal it to gamble. I used that money to pay our bills. It made me angry that I had to act like a parent when I was still a child myself.

But now that she was gone, I missed her. A lot. There were a lot of conflicting emotions and memories and it was difficult to sift through it all. So even though I wanted to think rationally about the loan shark, I couldn't.

As I got out of the shower, I heard knocking on the door. "Just a second!" I shouted. It was probably my neighbor, Mrs. Kimble. Our mail kept getting mixed up so she was probably just giving me some of my things that ended up in her mailbox.

I wrapped the towel around myself and opened the door. But instead of Mrs. Kimble on the other side, a middle-aged man was there. He was dressed in a cheap, tacky suit and his hair was slicked back and oily. He looked at me and leered as his eyes went down to the towel. I held it tighter to my chest. "Can I help you?"

"You must be Tris," he said. "I'm sorry to hear about your mother's passing. My name is Zack. I'm an old friend of hers."

"You're the loan shark, aren't you?"

His grin widened. It made my skin crawl. "So you've heard about me, then."

"My mother is dead."

"But I still don't have the 15 grand she owes me, so you can see we have a bit of a problem."

"15? The note said 10!"

"With interest."

"I don't have your money. Go away or I'll call the police." I tried to close the door but he slapped his hand on the door, stopping it in its tracks. He was strong. Even though he looked perfectly relaxed, I couldn't budge the door.

"Don't worry, Tris. I'll leave. But I will be coming for my money, one way or another." He looked down at me, dressed in only the skimpy towel, and smirked. "If you need extra employment to earn it then I'm sure something can be arranged."

"I'll get it. Please leave," I whispered.

He let go of the door and I slammed it and locked it. The towel fell to the ground and I realized my hands were shaking so hard that they couldn't hold the towel. "Fuck," I whispered.

I needed to get that money and fast. Which meant only one thing: I had to take out a loan from a bank. I didn't know if I was able to get that amount of money– my credit score was fine but it wasn't like I had any assets to use as collateral.

If I took out a personal loan, I would be paying that money back for years, but at least it would be from a bank and not a sleazy guy named Zack.

2

Dean

MIA, one of the bank tellers, came into my office. "Hey, Dean, there's someone here who wants to apply for a loan. She doesn't have an appointment. Should I tell her to come back after your lunch break?"

I glanced at the clock. It was already lunch? I had barely noticed where the time went. It didn't matter. I wasn't going to eat lunch anyway. I had too much work to do. "You can send her in now. Thank you."

Mia nodded and left. I took a sip of my coffee, trying to stay awake. I had been in the office since seven in the morning so I was feeling exhausted.

A young woman came into the office. She looked a little fearful but she gave me a hesitant smile.

"Hey," I said, smiling at her. "My name's Dean. Have a seat and we can go over your loan application."

"Thank you, sir. My name is Tris." She sat down and handed me a paper form that she had filled out.

"No need to call me sir," I said. I looked over the application. "Okay, so you want a personal loan for 15 grand. Wow. Are you getting married or going on vacation?"

She shook her head. "Neither."

I raised an eyebrow at her, expecting her to elaborate, but she didn't. She couldn't even meet my eyes. "What do you want the money for?"

"It's personal."

"Okay," I said slowly. Something was wrong. I could tell that. People were usually nervous when applying for a loan, but nothing like this. She was practically trembling. I debated asking her about it. I didn't want to scare her away, though. "Let me look up your credit history."

Her credit score was decent and she didn't have a lot of debt, only a small student loan that she had never missed a payment on. She didn't have any credit cards or anything else. It didn't make sense that she was taking about a loan of this size. "Do you have any assets that you could use as collateral?" I asked.

"No. I have a car, but it's twenty years old. It's probably not worth much."

"What about any property?"

She flinched. "I guess I do have my mom's house. She just passed away. I haven't had her place appraised yet."

"I'm sorry for your loss. That must be hard."

"It's complicated. But thank you." She tried to manage a smile, but couldn't quite reach it.

"If this loan is for funeral expenses, then we have

some different loan options for you to look at. One with lower interest rates."

She shook her head. "Thank you, but no. I had just enough money in my savings to cover that. This is for something else." She looked away and crossed her arms protectively in front of her.

"Tris, this may be a little too personal, but are you in some kind of trouble?" I needed to know.

She looked up at me, surprised. "Not yet," she said. "But if I don't get that money, then I will be."

"Why don't you tell me what's going on?"

She bit her lip. "My mom has– had– a gambling problem. And she owes money to a loan shark. He paid me a visit today." She shuddered. "He said something bad would happen if I didn't give him the money. He said he could find me other employment." She grimaced. I could guess what type of employment he was thinking.

Unfortunately, I had a sinking feeling about who this loan shark was. "Did you get a name from him?"

"He said his name was Zack."

Fuck.

"Zack Napier," I said.

She frowned. "You know him?"

"He's my cousin." I hadn't spoken to him in years. We never got along. He was always an asshole but I never thought he would stoop this low. I sighed. "I'm really sorry, Tris."

"It's okay. We definitely can't choose our family." She gave a humorless laugh.

I looked through her loan application again. She was

financially responsible. She lived within her means, but her savings had been wiped out by funeral expenses. And even though she had a decent income, between her monthly expenses and current debt, she would be living dangerously close to living paycheck to paycheck, even if she only made minimum payments on the loan. Minimum payments with our standard interest rate would keep her swimming in debt for years.

I looked up at her. She was biting her lip, looking at me nervously. I sighed. "I have to be honest, you won't be in great financial shape if you take out this loan. You'll be signing up for years of debt. Let me talk to my cousin. Maybe I can get him to forgive the debt. Or at least make him realize he's being a dick."

"Do you think you can get him to forgive the debt?"

"I can try," I said with a slight smile. "I'll call you with an update within the next week, I promise."

"Thank you," she said. "Thank you so much."

"Don't thank me yet." I would be shocked if he actually did see reason. But it was worth a try.

3

———————

Tris

I TRIED to put the loan out of my mind for the next week. It was difficult but I needed to get things done. I couldn't just shirk my work and leave my mom's place to decay.

A couple of days after I talked with Dean, I was at my mom's house, bleaching the dishes that were left in the sink. With the windows open to let in some fresh air, the kitchen almost wasn't nauseating.

It felt good taking action. It made me feel like I was in control. My plan was to sell as much of my mom's belongings as I could. It wouldn't fetch much, but it was at least something that could go back to paying off the loan, whether it was from the bank or a loan shark.

It was going to be hard trying to tackle the living room with all of the pyramid scheme products, or her bedroom, which was full of personal belongings. But it would at least be easy to sell the dishes.

There was a knock on the door, making me jump. I looked out the window to see Zack outside. I backed away from the window, feeling the panic rise up in me. How did he always know where I was? Was he following me?

"Tris," he called. "Open up. If you're naked in there, I don't mind."

My skin crawled and my stomach lurched. I stayed still, hoping he would just go away. I didn't want to call the police and get them involved in this. It was too embarrassing.

Zack let out a comical groan. "I left a jacket in the living room last time I was there. I would like it back. Just let me in and I'll grab the jacket and be on my way."

I walked into the cluttered living room. Looking around, I found an old jean jacket slung on a chair. It definitely belonged to a man. I tried to wipe the thought of Zack sitting in the living with my mother, discussing terms and maybe even intimidating her. It was too late now. I couldn't think about it.

I made sure the door chain was in place before opening the door a crack and tossing the jacket out at him. "There," I said. "You have your jacket. Now please leave. I don't have your money."

"Oh, don't worry," Zack said. "I won't be bothering you again. I'm sure my cousin will be calling you soon to tell you the good news."

The knot in my stomach eased somewhat. "You forgave the loan?"

Zack tipped back his head and laughed. "Is that what he told you? Oh no, honey. No. Dean bought your loan from me. Only he bought it for twenty grand. He was pretty desperate to buy it." Zack looked me up and down with a grin. "Maybe he likes you. God knows he's too much of a workaholic to get a real date. He probably has something special planned for you."

The knot in my stomach tightened again. I tried to breathe and think rationally, but it was difficult with the way Zack was leering at me. "You're lying," I said. "He wouldn't do that." Of course, what did I really know? I had spent less than a half hour with Dean. But I wanted to trust him. I *needed* to trust him. There was no way he would just buy my loan like that... would he?

The loan shark smirked. "Ask him yourself. You'll find him at the office– the asshole's always there. Word to the wise, I've seen his internet history. He's into some pretty kinky shit. Likes his girlfriends to dress up like schoolgirls and wear diapers. You're definitely his type, but I would start wearing my hair in pigtails if I were you."

My mind went blank. It was unable to process this information. "Get off my property," I finally said. "I never want to see you again."

He started to back away, his hands up in surrender even though he had a cocky look on his face. "I'm going," He said. "Have fun."

I waited until he left and then I fished my cell phone out of my pocket. I needed to call Dean and get this sorted out.

4

Dean

FOR ONCE, I took a lunch break. I had to because my computer screen couldn't come into focus for me. I was so tired and exhausted from confronting my cousin. It had taken days of arguing and shouting before I finally agreed to buy the loan for twenty grand. That son of a bitch had swindled me and I had let it happen. I wasn't going to let Tris suffer. She was too nice and sweet to be trapped like that, just because her mother didn't know how to handle finances.

And Zack was an asshole. He would want something more than money from Tris.

Now I just had to call her and tell her the loan was forgiven. It wasn't completely the truth, but it might as well be. I certainly wasn't ever going to collect.

I took a walk to the local cafe, wanting to get some food before I called her. However, on the way there, my phone rang. It was her. "Tris?" I said. "I was just about to call you."

"Did you buy my loan from Zack?"

Shit. I was going to kick his ass. "He shouldn't have talked to you. Are you all right?"

"I'm fine. I don't think I'm going to see him again. But did pay twenty thousand dollars for my loan?" Her voice shook a little.

Of course she was scared. She probably thought I was going to harass her just like Zack. "Don't worry about it," I said. "I have no intention of collecting."

"But you just spent a lot of money on me," she said. "I'm not going to let you spend twenty thousand dollars on someone you don't even know!"

"I'm not letting you pay me back," I said firmly. "That's final, Tris."

She was silent for a second and then she said, timidly. "Is there some other way I can pay you back?"

I stopped walking, suddenly no longer in the mood for lunch. I probably wouldn't be able to stomach it. She sounded scared of me. I had a hunch about what Zack told her. And it wasn't good. "What did my cousin tell you about me?"

"He said a lot of things. He was probably just trying to mess with me. Look, if you don't want my money, fine. But I have to do something. Do you need someone to do housework? I could come over on weekends and after I'm done with work."

I rubbed my forehead. I knew she wasn't going to stop until I agreed to something. I understood it. I also hated feeling indebted to someone. But I also knew exactly what Zack said to her. I was going to kill that son of a bitch. "Okay," I said. "Housework is fine. Are you free tomorrow? We can grab lunch and discuss the details. I'll write up a contract as well."

"Is a contract really necessary?"

"Yes." The last thing I wanted was her worrying I would take advantage of her two months from now. A contract would make expectations clear.

"Okay," she said. "Lunch tomorrow sounds good. It's my day off anyway."

"Perfect. There's a cafe next to the bank. We'll meet there." After hanging up, I took a deep breath. I knew what Zack had told her. The last time he was at my house was for a family barbecue. He snuck onto my laptop and checked my search history and found out I was a Daddy. He gave me shit for it and I told him I never wanted to speak with him again. That was the last time I had talked to him before calling him about Tris. And it looked like he hadn't forgotten.

I just hope that whatever he told Tris hadn't scared her.

I met up with her the next day during lunch. She looked a little nervous but she smiled as she joined me at the table. A server came by and she ordered a small tea but no food. "You can get whatever you want," I said. "It's on me."

She shook her head. "I'd rather not," she said. "I already owe you a lot."

"It's really no trouble."

She looked down, her cheeks growing red. I remembered what Zack probably told her. She probably wanted to get out of here and away from me as quickly as possible. "Look," I said quietly. "I'm sure Zack said some unsavory things about me and he might have been pretty vulgar about it. But I don't want you to be scared of me. I won't hurt you."

"I believe you," she said. "I know he was just trying to scare me. I don't think he likes you very much."

I smirked. "Believe me, the feeling's mutual. But you don't have to worry about that anymore. He won't bother you again." And if he did, I really would kick his ass.

I pulled out a single piece of paper with a couple of paragraphs for terms. "Here's the contract," I said. "If you come in once a week and vacuum and do the laundry for three months, then we'll be square. Does that sound reasonable?"

She frowned. "That's way too little for twenty thousand dollars. At most that's two hours of work a week I should be doing more."

"I don't spend a lot of time at home," I said. "What little time I spend at home I usually spend cleaning. You would be freeing up a lot of time for me which is invaluable."

She looked skeptical but started looking over the contract, which said the terms completely. "It says I'll over come over when you're working. I'll need your schedule for that."

"Don't worry. I'm always working. Unless you come

over at ten at night, then I'll be working, I promise. You won't even have to see me."

She smiled slightly. "Yeah, half of the contract seems to just be saying that."

"I don't want to make you uncomfortable," I said. "So it'll be easier if I'm just out of the way."

"It's your own home," she said. "I don't want to banish you from there." She took out a pen and started making changes to the contract. "And I'll come by every day after work to wash dishes."

"Absolutely not. That's too much."

"You just saved me from a loan shark. I don't think it's too much at all."

I gritted my teeth. I didn't want her to feel indebted to me because of that. All I did was do damage control for my family. It was something I was used to. But I wasn't going to convince her of that. "I don't have a lot of dirty dishes because I don't cook. So you can come in three times a week to do dishes."

Her eyes lit up. "Then I can make you dinner. That would be perfect! Five times a week I can come by and wash the dishes and make you dinner. And then on the weekends I'll vacuum and do the laundry."

I smiled and shook my head. "I'm pretty sure you're supposed to negotiate for less work. Not more work."

She bit her lip. "Look, when my mom wasn't chasing pyramid schemes or gambling, she spent her time arguing with debt collectors and trying to borrow money from family members. I hated watching it and seeing what it did to her and the family. Because of her, I haven't seen my aunts or uncles since I was little. I only started speaking to my grandparents again after I turned eighteen. I told myself I wasn't going to become like her. I wasn't going to be indebted to anyone. I'm not going to start now. So please, just let me do this."

Slowly, I nodded. As much as I hated it, I understood. "Okay," I said. "You have a deal."

5

Tris

AFTER MAKING the deal with Dean, I didn't see him again for weeks. He had stayed true to his word about not being at home. Even though I had crossed it out of the contract, he was determined not to see me. He was probably as embarrassed about the whole thing as I was.

I didn't mind doing housework for him. It was really easy, especially compared to my mother's house.

He had a large two-story house all to himself. It was the most organized house I had ever been in. He kept his laundry in a hamper outside his bedroom and any dirty dishes were already rinsed and put in the dish washer before I arrived. The work was minimal.

But I enjoyed it anyway. It kept me from feeling indebted. I knew my debt would be paid off in three months and that would be it. And I had to admit, I was curious about Dean.

He was really sexy. I knew that from the beginning. And he was incredibly kind. Also, I couldn't stop thinking about what Zack had said, about his type. The more I thought about it, the more I liked the thought of wearing pigtails and a cute little schoolgirl outfit for him.

Even though I was in his debt, he made me feel safe. I wasn't used to that. It usually took me awhile to trust someone. But not Dean. I trusted him almost immediately.

So I enjoyed cleaning his house because it gave me insight into his life that few people would get. I never went snooping, of course. But I looked at the photographs in his living room. There were only a few of them of him and his parents, but they were all from when he was younger. On the walls there were a few paintings which made the place feel homey, but that was it.

In one corner of the living room was a bookshelf. Most of the books looked like they had only been read once or twice, but the books on the bottom had been read thoroughly, over and over. They looked like children's books, probably childhood favorites. I smiled and took time to read over the titles once. A lot of them were my favorites from childhood as well. I had forgotten about a lot of them so it was nice for the reminder, even if I didn't have a lot of time for reading these days. Between my regular job, cleaning my mom's place, and doing housework for Dean, I barely found time to eat and sleep, much less read.

Two weeks into the deal with Dean, I was busy cooking him spaghetti and meatballs to leave for him. I was exhausted. I had gotten up early to try to clean some of

Mom's bedroom before work. I ended up crying on her bedroom floor. That left me drained and distracted for the rest of the day. Somehow I had muddled through work, but now my vision was blurring a little as I shaped the meatballs together. I blinked rapidly. My day was almost over. I was so close. I could do this. I just needed to concentrate.

I wobbled a little and barely caught myself before I fell down. "Shit," I whispered. Okay. Maybe I needed to sit down. Just for a couple of minutes.

I slid down to the ground, feeling immediate relief in my feet from sitting. I closed my eyes, which still felt a little itchy from all the crying earlier. I just needed a couple of seconds and then I would be all right. Just a couple...

I must have fallen asleep because the next thing I knew I was being shook awake by a strong hand. "Tris?" Dean said. "Come on, wake up for me."

My eyes fluttered open and I looked up to see his concerned face only inches away from my own. I looked away, blushing. "Did I fall asleep? What time is it?" My eyes widened. "Shit. The meatballs."

I tried to get up but he grabbed my arms and held me still. "Oh, no you don't," he said. "I can get my own dinner for the night. Stay there. Let me get you some water. Did you fall down? Does your head hurt?"

I rubbed my eyes, trying to wake up. "No, I sat down," I said. "I'm fine. Just a little tired. I'm so sorry, I didn't mean to fall asleep."

He gave me a glass of water and knelt next to me on

the ground. "Drink this. I have a guest room. You can spend the night here."

I sipped the water, but then shook my head. "No. I can't. That's way too much trouble..."

"I'm not letting you drive home like this. If you would prefer, I'll drive you home. But I don't want you passing out behind the wheel."

I didn't know which would be worse. But I knew he was exhausted from work and had just gotten home. I didn't want him to go out again. "I'll stay," I said weakly. "Thank you."

He looked me up and down, his brow furrowing. "You've lost weight since the last time I saw you. Have you been eating?"

"When I have time."

He raised an eyebrow. "How often is that?"

I shrugged.

He scoffed. "You've been cooking dinner for me every night but you haven't been feeding yourself?"

I bit my lip. It sounded silly when he said it like that.

Dean sighed and stood up. "Stay there. I'm going to fix you something to eat."

"No, you really–"

"Don't argue with me."

Something about his tone made me close my mouth immediately and shut up. "Yes, sir," I whispered.

"No." He pinched the bridge of his nose. "I'm sorry. You don't have to call me sir or... or anything else. I shouldn't have spoken like that. I'm just worried about you. If I knew you were overworking yourself like this I never would have let you."

"It was my choice. I need to pay off the debt."

He ignored me and opened his freezer and pulled out a small frozen pizza. "I know this isn't as good as what you usually cook for me, but it's the best I can do on short notice." He started preheating the oven and then reached out his hand to me. "Come on. Let's get you onto the couch."

I took his hand and he pulled me to my feet. The room started spinning and I collapsed into his chest. He wrapped his arms around me and I noticed how muscular he was beneath his button-down shirt. He was strong and it made me feel protected. All I wanted to do was relax and let him take care of me. *How embarrassing..*

Dean picked me up and carried me to the couch in the living room. I leaned against his shoulder, not saying anything. I knew I should be protesting and insisting I could walk on my own. But I couldn't. I didn't have the energy.

He set me down on the couch. "Just relax," he said. "I'll give you the pizza as soon as it's ready. Then you can eat and off to bed, okay?"

I nodded weakly. I couldn't find the energy to speak.

It didn't take long for him to give me the pizza and another glass of water. "Eat and drink," he said.

I realized he wasn't eating anything. "What about you?"

"I'll fix something for myself after I get you tucked into bed."

I frowned but he raised an eyebrow, daring me to argue. I decided against it and ate my food. I didn't realize how hungry I was until I took the first bite. I wolfed down the rest of the food, sighing with satisfaction at the end. When was the last time I sat down for a proper meal? In my exhausted state, I couldn't even remember.

"Drink." He commanded. I drank the water in one gulp. He smiled grimly. "Good girl."

I felt my face flush even as a shiver of pleasure ran down my spin. Whoa. What was that reaction? I didn't even know what to think about it.

Dean's face was unreadable. He set my empty plate and glass aside and picked me up. "Time to take you to bed."

The only rooms in Dean's house I had not been in were his bedroom. He told me not to clean in there. Normally I would be really curious about what the guest room looked like, but I could barely keep my eyes open, especially now that my stomach was full.

He set me down on a soft bed and pulled a comforter up over me. I was already drifting off as soon as my head hit the pillow. I thought I heard him say "Sleep well, baby girl," but I might have just imagined it.

6

———

Dean

I WAS IN TROUBLE. I had been so careful to avoid Tris. I knew if I spent any amount of time with her, I would develop feelings for her. And I didn't want to make her uncomfortable.

But because I had been avoiding her, I didn't realize she had been overworking herself to honor our deal. I was an idiot.

The next morning, I woke up before Tris did. It was a Saturday so neither of us were working. Normally I would do a little bit of work in the office anyway, but not today. Today I had to take care of Tris, whether or not she liked it.

I decided to make her an omelet with bacon for breakfast. As I prepared it, I tried to consider my best move from here. My Daddy voice had accidentally come out when I was speaking to her yesterday. I couldn't help it, not when I saw her so vulnerable. I was so scared she had passed out and needed to go to the hospital. But she had responded so beautifully to it.

She had submitted immediately and blushed. She looked so adorable. And maybe I was fooling myself, but it looked like she even enjoyed it a little.

It was obvious the original deal couldn't continue, contract or not. She would end up in the hospital at this rate. And I never meant to overwork her when I signed that deal.

I would let her out of the contract and forgive the debt in a heartbeat if I thought she would let me. That's what I wanted to do in the first place anyway.

But if she insisted on paying me back, then the terms of the contract would have to change. What I wanted more than anything was to make her my Little. But would she agree to that? Or would I scare her away for good?

I guess there was only one way to find out.

When breakfast was cooked, I put the food on a plate and carried it upstairs with a glass of orange juice. I knocked on the door softly. "Tris? Are you awake?"

"Come in," she said.

I opened the door to see her looking up at me sleepily. She barely lifted her head to look at me. She looked a little more rested but her face was pale. I wouldn't be surprised if she was getting sick. "How did you sleep?" I asked.

"Very well. In a few minutes I can get up to do laundry. I promise."

"Absolutely not." I set her breakfast down on the

nightstand next to her bed. "The first thing I need from you is to eat. And then we need to talk." I pulled up a small armchair and sat down next to her bed.

She looked at the food, her eyes wide. "I thought you couldn't cook."

"I said I don't cook. Not can't." I shrugged. "I don't like cooking when it's just for myself. It's more enjoyable to cook for someone else. I just wish it was under better circumstances and not because you passed out on me."

She bit her lip as she looked at me nervously. "I'm sorry I fell asleep last night. It won't happen again. I promise."

"You're right," I said. "It won't. Because I'm not going to let you clean for me anymore."

Tris's eyes widened. "But the contract–"

"The contract is killing you. We need to change it."

She frowned a little but she sat up to start eating her food. I was happy to see her eat. She clearly needed it. It had only been a couple of weeks but she must have lost at least ten pounds in that time. She was pushing herself to the brink. That needed to end now.

Tris finished eating and drank the orange juice. Once she was done, she looked a little more alert. She leaned against the headboard of the bed. "Yesterday was just a bad day," she said. "I was pushed myself harder than I should have, you're right. But it was the exception. Not the norm."

"If you don't slow down, it'll become the norm."

"I can't slow down. I have debts to pay, work to do, and

my mom's house to..." she trailed off and swallowed. "To tend to."

I couldn't even imagine the emotional strain she was feeling right now. "You don't have to do this by yourself," I said. "Let me help."

She shook her head. "No. I already owe you too much."

"No. You don't."

She huffed. "You spent twenty thousand dollars on me."

"Yes, because it was my cousin. I had to."

"I still need to pay you back."

I sighed. "Well, I'm not going to let you clean my house like before. There's two options. The first option is the deal is off. Your debt is forgiven and we go our separate ways."

"What's the second option?"

I took a deep breath. "The second option is you move in with me for a few months. You let me take care of you and help you with your mom's place. All you would have to do is follow a few simple rules like being in bed on time and cleaning up after yourself. I'll take care of everything else. I'll even cook you food. Just seeing you relax and recover would be payment enough."

She bit her lip and conflict crossed her features. I knew she was thinking of saying something but was worried about saying it. I had a feeling I knew what she was thinking.

"Talk to me," I said. "Whatever it is, you can say it." It was time to get it out in the open.

"When Zack talked to me, he said you liked certain things. That you liked your girlfriends to wear pigtails and diapers and school girl outfits."

I nodded. "That's true," I said. "I won't lie to you. I do like those things. But I wouldn't ever make you do those things. The last thing I want is for you to be uncomfortable. And again, if you want, I can forgive the debt and we can go our separate ways."

Tris hugged her knees to her chest. She looked absolutely adorable and so vulnerable. It was difficult for me to tell what she was thinking. She didn't look disgusted with me. That was something at least. "Zack also said I was your type," she said, blushing a little. "Is that true? Would you want... want me in pigtails?"

I needed to kill Zack. "Yes," I admitted. "I want you to be my Little. But I wouldn't ever ask you to do that. I wouldn't ever expect it from you."

She was blushing harder now. "I wouldn't mind it," she said. She wouldn't look at me, instead staring at her feet.

I really wanted this to be real. I wanted to be her Daddy. But I remembered our lunch two weeks ago, when she insisted on taking more work because she felt guilty. I couldn't let her become my Little out of a sense of obligation. "No," I said. "I only want you to be my Little because you want to be. Not for any other reason. Not because of some stupid debt."

"I want to," she said. "Please." She blushed harder but she forced herself to look at me. "After Zack told me that, I couldn't get it out of my head. I've never really thought about it before, but I like the idea."

She sounded sincere. It gave me room to hope. "It's more than just wearing pigtails and cute clothes," I said. "You would act innocent and carefree, like a little kid. You would color and read children's books and watch children's movies. And you would call me Daddy. Are you sure you want to do that?"

She nodded. "Yes," she said. "Yes, Daddy."

Fuck. It sounded so good when I heard her say those words. I smiled. "Good girl, baby girl."

She smiled when I said that and blushed. She was so cute.

"How are you feeling?"

"Sleepy," she admitted. "But I slept all last night."

"You've put yourself through a lot," I said. "You need time to recover. How about you get some more sleep, okay? Can you do that for me, baby girl?"

"Yes, Daddy," she said, lying down and putting the blanket over her.

"Good girl."

After she was settled down, with her eyes closed, I left the room, feeling happy. I couldn't believe she had agreed to become my Little.

7

Tris

It FELT good having Dean be my Daddy. I felt safe with him. Even if I wasn't sure what to do. Even if he did enjoy my company and taking care of me, it still felt like I was getting the better end of the deal. After all, I got to rest and relax while he took care of me.

After a short nap, I was feeling even better. I still felt sleepy. I definitely wasn't up for going to my mom's house, even though that was my plan after finishing the housework at Dean's place. But it looked like that was all changed now.

And that was probably for the best. My throat felt a little sore when I woke up. And as I got out of bed, I started to cough. I groaned. Of course, I was getting sick now.

When I started to cough, Dean appeared in the doorway, looking at me with concern. "I'm fine," I croaked out.

"The next time you lie to me, I'll punish you, baby girl," he said. He strode over to me and put his hand on my forehead. His hand felt cool. "You have a slight fever," he said. "I'm not surprised you're sick with the way you were running yourself ragged."

"I don't want to go back to bed. I just got up. I can't spend all day in bed."

He gave me a slight smirk. "You don't have to stay in bed all day," he said. "You're going to spend all day on the couch in the living room."

I made a face but I was too tired to argue. Besides, I knew he was right.

He grabbed my hand and pulled me close to him. I leaned into his chest. He was so strong. "I know you're not used to someone taking care of you," he whispered in my ear. "But you agreed to let me. That especially applies to when you're sick."

"I don't know," I said uncertainly.

"Do you want to be my Little?" he pulled back, looking at me with concern. "If you don't, that's okay. But if you're my Little then you have to let me take care of you."

I nodded. "Yes, Daddy," I said. "I want to be your Little. I'm sorry. I'm not used to this. I've been taking care of myself ever since I was a kid."

He ran his fingers through my hair. The feeling felt good and strangely comforting. "Then it's about time someone took care of you," he whispered.

"Yes, Daddy."

He led me into the living room and had me sit down on the couch. Dean grabbed a blanket and put it over me before disappearing back upstairs. He came back with a stuffy. "Here," He said, handing it to me. "Cuddle it. It'll make you feel better."

The stuffy was a penguin. It was absolutely adorable. I smiled and hugged it to my chest. Something inside me relaxed. I hadn't held a stuffy in forever. I forgot how soft and comforting it felt.

Dean turned on the TV and handed me the remote. "Put on your favorite movie," he said. "You get to watch your favorite movie when you're sick."

"Thank you, Daddy."

"It's my pleasure, baby girl."

As I flipped through the movie selections on the streaming service, Dean disappeared again, only to come back with some hot tea. "This has honey and lemon in it," he said. "It'll help with your throat. I'm going to run to the store to get some medicine for you."

"Thank you, Daddy," I said.

He smiled and leaned down to kiss my forehead. "My pleasure, baby girl," he said.

After he left, I decided to watch *Cinderella*. I hadn't watched that movie in decades, but I remember enjoying it.

And right now I felt a little like Cinderella, getting pampered and spoiled by the prince after being rescued from her stepmother. Dean acted like taking care of me was the most natural thing in the world. But I had never experienced anything like this before.

Even when I was little, I knew that if I didn't do chores, they wouldn't get done. My mother certainly wasn't going to do them. So even when I was home sick from school, I had to do the dishes and laundry. Mom was usually out gambling or maybe sleeping off a hangover, so I would make myself tea and get myself medicine even though I needed to stand on a chair and a stack of books to reach the medicine cabinet. This felt... unnatural. Like a dream. Nothing like real life.

I hugged the stuffy tighter to me as I watched the movie. But as I did so, I felt sad. Inexplicably sad. Tears streamed down my face as I watched Cinderella dance with her prince.

I barely heard the front door open. But when Dean entered the room, I tried to brush the tears away before he could see. However, it was too late.

"Hey," he whispered. "It's okay. It's okay, baby girl." He grabbed me and held me tight to him. "Shh. It's okay."

"I don't even know why I'm crying."

"It's okay. You don't need to know. Not right now." He rubbed circles on my back while I cried. The tears turned into full-blown sobs, but he didn't care. He just held me tightly, whispering reassurances in my ear. "It's okay, baby girl," he said. "It's okay, I promise."

Slowly, I stopped crying and became very quiet. My mind felt quiet too. I wasn't thinking about anything. I was too tired to think.

Dean held me for several more seconds until he was sure I was calm. "Was it the movie?" he asked.

I shook my head.

"Was it because I left?"

I shook my head again.

He ran his hand through my hair. "Do you know what it was, baby girl?"

"I was just thinking about how this felt so strange to me. When I was little, I had to take care of myself when I was sick. I can't remember a time my mom made me tea for a sore throat or anything like that. It just made me cry."

He held me tighter to him. "I'm sorry, baby girl," he said. "You deserved better. You deserved to have someone take care of you. You never should have gone through that." He kissed the top of my head. It felt nice. "I'm here now," he said. "I'll take care of you for as long as you want me to, okay? Because you deserve it."

I clutched at his shirt and buried my face in his chest as if I was a small child. "Thank you, Daddy."

"You're welcome, baby girl."

I had to turn away suddenly to cough. One cough turned into a whole coughing fit.

Dean reached for the shopping bag he had dropped on the floor. "Hang on, baby girl. I have your medicine right here." He pulled out a small bottle of cold medicine and poured me a capful. "Drink. All of it."

I swallowed it down quickly, wincing at the harsh taste. But it still made me feel a little better almost immediately. My irritated throat was soothed a little. "Thank you, Daddy."

"I have something else for you," he said. He reached into the bag and pulled out a pajama set. It came with soft flannel pants and a matching shirt. "You'll be more comfy in these. We'll pick up your clothes and everything else you need tomorrow but I wanted to be more comfortable as soon as possible."

I looked down and realized I was still in my jeans and ratty t-shirt from yesterday. I was so out of it, I had completely forgotten what clothes I was wearing. "Changing sounds good. Thank you, Daddy."

He handed me the clothes and I ran into the bathroom to change. When I came back out, he was already making me another cup of tea. "Feel better, baby girl?" he asked with a smile.

I nodded. "Yes, Daddy. I feel much, much better."

His grin broadened. "Good. I'm glad, baby girl. Now go back to the couch. I'll bring you some more tea in just a minute."

I bit my lip. I shouldn't ask him to do something for me. Not when he was already doing so much. But I wanted to ask. "Could you maybe watch a movie with me, Daddy?" I asked.

He nodded. "Absolutely, baby girl. If that's what you want."

I nodded. "Yes, Daddy. Please."

"Go into the living room. I'll just be a minute."

I went into the living room and made room on the couch for him. I wanted to cuddle up next to him while we watched something. It might be a little forward of me. After all, we barely knew each other and I had only started being his Little this morning. But he made me feel safe. He was so patient with me when I was crying and he was so comforting. Now I just wanted to cuddle up next to him.

8

____

Dean

I JOINED Tris in the living room after making her tea. I handed it to her and she smiled up at me. She was already looking so much better than before.

It had been surprising to come back from the store to see her crying. I hated the thought of her crying alone, without someone to comfort her. Especially when she never had someone to comfort her and take care of her the way she should have been.

That would change now. Now she had me to take care of her.

Once I was settled on the couch, she started a movie. It was *Sleeping Beauty*. She curled up next to me, resting her head on my arm. I smiled. I loved having her in this position. It made me wonder how she would feel if put my arm around her and pulled her closer to me. But I was happy she felt so comfortable around me.

But as amazing as it felt having her cuddled up against me, I started to feel antsy. I had left plenty of work to do at the office. I couldn't remember the last time I hadn't gone in for even a few hours on the weekend. I was happy I was spending time with Tris and taking care of her, but my mind kept wandering to all of the things I needed to do at the bank. There was a movie producer, Christopher Murphy, who was coming to town, and he was looking for funding for his movie. I had been working with him in helping secure funding...

"Daddy?"

I looked down to see Tris staring up at me with wide eyes. "Yes, baby girl?"

"We can switch to a different movie if you're bored."

I felt a stab of guilt. Of course, she would notice I was distracted. I should have been paying attention to her. "No, I'm not bored, baby girl." I gave her a weak smile. "I guess I'm as used to sitting still as you are."

"Oh yeah, you usually do work on the weekends. Do you need to go in today?"

I thought about the tasks I have sitting on my desk. Technically, none of them had a deadline until the end of Monday. "I suppose not," I said.

She nodded. "It's easy to get distracted with work," she said. "You're going to burn yourself out if you're not careful." She blushed. "Not that I'm one to talk."

I smiled and hugged her closer to me. "You're right, baby girl," I said. "I should be more careful. I tell you what– I won't go to work on the weekends anymore. And I'll be home at six instead of ten."

She smiled. "Good."

I kissed the top of her head. "I have to be. After all, I have something much more important than work waiting for me right here."

It was hard, but I managed to put work out of my mind for a while and enjoy the time with Tris. We spent the day watching movies together and relaxing. I made us lunch and dinner. After a day of rest and full meals, Tris was already starting to look better, even though she would probably have a cold for a few more days.

A couple of hours after dinner, she was starting to fall asleep on the couch. I gently nudged her awake. "Okay, baby girl," I said. "It's time to get you to bed."

"Yes, Daddy."

I picked her up and she rested her head against my shoulder. I smiled as I carried her up to her bed. I was glad she had taken so well to me carrying her like this. I could do it all day without getting tired.

I set her down gently on her bed. Her eyes fluttered open as she looked at me. "Daddy? Can you stay with me tonight?"

I wanted to, more than anything. But I hesitated. Was she really ready for this? "Are you sure, baby girl?"

She nodded. "I want you to, Daddy. Please."

I smoothed her hair away from her face. "Okay, baby girl. I'm happy to stay with you."

I lied down in bed next to her and wrapped my arm around her waist, hugging her close to me. "Is this okay, baby girl?"

"It's perfect, Daddy. Thank you."

I smiled and kissed her temple. "I'm glad, baby girl. Sleep tight."

Together, we drifted off to sleep.

The next morning, we both woke up around nine. I was feeling better and more at peace than I had felt in a long time. It felt good to be holding my cute Little in my arms, especially after a day of rest. It was going to be difficult to adjust to a more reasonable work schedule, but it would be worth it, especially when I had to take care of my Little.

I commanded Tris to stay in bed while I went to make us both breakfast. I decided on toast and fruit this morning. I got coffee for myself but herbal tea with honey for her. I went back upstairs and handed her the breakfast, along with her drink. "After breakfast, I'll get you your medicine," I said. "And then we'll go to your place and you can pack whatever you need to stay here."

"I should also go to my mom's place," she said. "Just to do a little bit of cleaning. I know I can't push myself but the sooner I get it over with, the better."

I thought about it for a second. I knew she wanted to get back to work. But she needed to rest. And cleaning out her mom's place would be a struggle for her. "Next week," I said. "Next weekend we'll go over to your mom's place."

9

Tris

A WEEK LATER, we drove to my mom's house. I couldn't help but feel nervous about Dean seeing my mom's place. After a week of living with him, I felt comfortable with him in most circumstances. He had been patient and affectionate without being pushy. Even though we slept in the same bed every night, he only ever kissed my forehead. He was so careful to make sure I felt safe and cared for, and that meant the world to me.

But I was still nervous. His house was immaculate. Even before I started cleaning, there was very little for me to do. Everything was orderly, without so much as a stray sock on the floor.

My mom's house was the exact opposite of that.

Luckily, after a week of pampering, I was more or less healthy again. Even though both of us worked during the week, Dean made sure I took my medicine and spent all of my free time relaxing. He even drew me a bubble bath one night to help me stay fully relaxed. That was good because it was going to take all of my strength to show Dean this hell hole.

"This isn't the house I grew up in," I said as we approached the house. "Mom downsized after I graduated. For better or worse, I guess."

"Are you sure you're ready to do this?" he asked. His brow was furrowed in concern. "We can wait another week if you want."

"No," I said. "I need to do this. I need to get this over with."

Together, we entered the house. It already looked better than when I first got it. The kitchen was clean and practically functional again and the gross musty smell that permeated the house was weaker now. It would take a while for it to be fully gone, but at least the air was breathable.

I led the way to the living room, which was still as messy as ever and full of pyramid scheme products. I needed to start here today or I would never clean out this room.

I snuck a peek at Dean when we entered the living room. His face was unreadable as he looked around. "What is all of this?" he asked. "Was your mom in the middle of moving?"

"Worse," I said. I opened up one of the boxes to reveal cheap, poorly made leggings. "She was in the middle of a get-rich-quick scheme. She always was."

He grimaced. "Those never end well."

"She was involved in all of them. I remember leggings, health shakes, and makeup the most. The last one was essential oils." I swallowed as I glared down at an innocent-looking box barely visible behind the ratty armchair. "That's probably where most of the money she borrowed from Zack went."

Dean started looking through the products. "I recognize a lot of these," he said. "You'd be surprised about how many people try to take out business loans to fund these ventures. They're denied, of course, but pictures of most of these products have crossed my desk at least once."

"I have no idea what I'm going to do with them," I said. "I considered selling these for pennies online but I can't stomach the thought."

"Some of these are dangerous anyway," Dean said, picking up a case of cheap eye shadow. A look of disgust crossed his face. "This company blinded someone if I remember right." He shook his head. "You need to throw all of this out. I can help you."

I nodded. "Please."

Together, we loaded boxes and boxes of crap into his car. We drove it to the local trash drop-off site and went back to the house. After a couple of more trips, the living room looked functional again.

I stared at the ratty armchairs and the TV. The rug was stained and dingy and the chairs had rips in them. But the living room looked almost comfy without all of the crap in there. I thought I would feel better when it was gone, but somehow I felt even worse knowing Mom probably never sat comfortably in this living room. She was always drowning in boxes. I swallowed. "Let's go," I said. "That's enough for today."

"Okay," Dean said quietly. "How does ice cream sound?"

I smiled weakly at him. "That sounds wonderful, Daddy. Thank you."

We were both quiet as we drove to get ice cream. I felt sick to my stomach after looking through all of that junk and I was also embarrassed Dean saw it. He was nice, of course. But he had to be disgusted with it all.

"Thank you," I finally said. "Thank you for coming with me. I know that wasn't the most pleasant time."

"I'm glad I could be there for you," he said.

"Yeah, but the place is gross and cluttered and dingy. It probably looks even worse from your perspective."

The corner of his mouth quirked up. "Are you calling me a neat freak?"

I smiled softly. "I never said it was a bad thing."

"Honestly, my house looked similar when I was growing up," He said quietly.

I looked at him, surprised. "Really?"

He nodded. "My family was– is— a wreck. I'll spare you the details, but let's just say Zack fits in better than I do." He grimaced. "I'm probably the only one who hasn't been arrested at least once. Nothing was ever in good working condition in my house. That included both the family and the house itself. I haven't spoken to them in years. I did everything I could to make sure I didn't end up in that situation. That's probably why I threw myself into my work the way I did. But the point is I understand. I wouldn't ever judge you for what your mom's house looked like."

I smiled, feeling a little reassured. I leaned my head against his shoulder. "Thank you, Daddy."

"You don't have to thank me for that, baby girl."

10

Dean

THAT NIGHT after we got ice cream and went back home, Tris changed into her pajamas and met me in the living room. Her hair was done up into pigtails and she was hugging a stuffy to her chest. I knew she was in Little space. She was probably trying to recover from the day. I smiled and grabbed her hand, pulling her towards me. I kissed the top of her head. "How do chicken tenders and french fries sound for dinner?" I asked. "I think you've earned a little treat for being such a good girl today."

She smiled and bounced up and down in excitement. "Thank you, Daddy!" she said.

"My pleasure, baby girl. Now go wash up. It'll be ready, shortly." I turned to start preparing dinner.

"Hey, Daddy?" she said shyly.

I looked back at her, surprised to see her biting her lip

nervously. She hadn't done that since the first day of being my Little. "Yes, baby girl?"

"C-can I kiss you, Daddy?"

The simple question sent heat through me. "Are you sure you're ready for that, baby girl?" I asked.

She nodded. "I want to. I've actually wanted to kiss you for a while now. Can I please kiss you?"

I strode over to her and cupped her face with my palm. She leaned into my touch, her eyes fluttering closed with pleasure. I lowered my face towards her and pressed my lips against hers. She sighed and wrapped her arms around my waist as she leaned into the kiss. My cock grew hard and I groaned. I licked her bottom lip, demanding entry. She parted her lips, letting me in. I explored her mouth with my tongue. My cock grew hard. I knew I wasn't going to be able to stop myself unless I stopped now. I broke off with a groan. "You taste so sweet, baby girl," I whispered to her.

She smiled. "I'm glad, Daddy."

I leaned my head against her shoulder, trying to get a hold of myself. "If I hadn't stopped myself, I probably would have lifted you onto the kitchen counter and taken you for myself."

She giggled. "I'm sad you stopped then."

Heat rushed through me at her words. I kissed her once more on the lips. "After dinner," I said. "If you still want to, I'll take you up to my room after dinner."

She pouted but nodded. "Yes, Daddy."

However, all through dinner, there was only one thing

I could think of and that was getting my sweet little girl on my bed and under me.

She seemed to be thinking the exact same thing because as soon as dinner was over, she practically skipped up the stairs to my room. I grinned as I followed her upstairs.

By the time I reached my room, she was already perched on my bed. "I'm all ready, Daddy," she said.

I smiled. "Then lie down on the bed for me, baby girl."

She grinned and lied down. I got on top of her and kissed her. Balancing my weight on one elbow, I used my free hand to explore her body, feeling her soft, perky breasts through the thin fabric of her t-shirt before going down to her pajama pants. I slipped a hand inside her and found her bare pussy underneath. I groaned. "Naughty girl," I growled. "Not wearing any underwear."

She giggled. "It's uncomfy, Daddy."

I trailed kisses down her body, over her t-shirt, and down to her hips. Gently, I peeled off her pants, revealing her bare pussy underneath.

I groaned as I looked at it. It was practically soaked. I traced a finger over her slit and she shuddered from the sensation. "You're ready for me, aren't you, baby girl?" I whispered. "You're all ready for Daddy's cock?"

"Yes, Daddy," she whimpered. "I want your cock so badly."

I smiled. "Well, you'll have to be patient."

She whined as I pulled my fingers away from her pussy but I hushed her by pressing a finger against her lips. I took off her t-shirt, revealing her breasts to me. I gazed down at her, naked on my bed. She was so fucking beautiful.

I leaned down to kiss her again as I started to play with her breast, teasing her nipple into a hard point. She moaned and bucked her hips with need. I trailed kisses down her neck as my hand trailed down her body, back to her pussy. I thrust my fingers inside her. She was so wet and needy, her body practically sucked my fingers into her. I grinned. She was ready for me. I straightened up and unbuttoned my pants, pulling out my hard cock. She looked at me hungrily. "Are you ready for me, baby girl?" I asked, stroking my cock.

"Yes, Daddy," she whispered.

I placed my cock at her entrance and slowly pushed in. She cried out with pleasure as I entered and I groaned as I buried my face in the crook of her neck. She felt so good. She felt like absolute heaven.

Tris's breathing grew heavier and more urgent as she bucked her hips. I put my thumb on her clit, teasing her. "I want you to come for me, baby girl," I growled as I thrust harder into her. "I want you to come all over your Daddy's cock."

"Yes, Daddy," she moaned.

I kept teasing her and thrusting into her until suddenly her entire body stiffened up and she came all over my cock.

The force of her orgasm was enough to make me come as well and I let out a shuddering groan. "Fuck," I whispered.

Slowly, I pulled out of her, looking at how my hot seed

leaked out of her sweet, little pussy. Tris sighed softly, exhausted from her orgasm. "I'm going to get all messy, Daddy," she said.

I smiled. "I think I have just the thing, baby girl." I went to my closet and pulled out a package of adult diapers. I held one up for her. "You said panties weren't comfy. Let's see how this feels."

She smiled and nodded, lifting up her hips so I could put it on her.

I slid the diaper under her and fashioned it into place. "How does that feel, baby girl?"

She wiggled her hips, getting used to it. "It feels good, Daddy," she said, smiling.

I grinned and kissed her forehead. "You look absolutely adorable wearing it," I said. I got into bed beside her and gathered her up into my arms. "Are you okay, baby girl? I know things happened really fast."

"Couldn't be better." She closed her eyes and smiled as she snuggled up against me. "I feel safe with you, Daddy. I loved every second of it and I feel wonderful right now."

I smiled. "I'm glad to hear that, baby girl." I held her even tighter to me. "You're beautiful and I'm so happy you're mine. My Little."

Call to Action

Dean and Tris are on their way to living happily ever after. Aren't they cute for each other? What will happen with the mysterious movie producer coming to town? Will

Christopher find love? Find out in *Charismatic Producer Daddy*.

Charismatic Producer Daddy book description:

She was in his debt. He wanted her.

Anna

All I wanted was a little extra money.

I thought it would be easy when I answered the casting call for extras.

How hard would it be to act natural in the background?

Unfortunately, my acting debut ended with a freak accident and a trip to the hospital.

Lost work time and medical bills on top of that would leave me in debt for years.

But then Christopher, one of the producers, steps in as if it's nothing.

He pays my bills and takes care of me.

Immediately, I feel safe with him.

He's protective of me and incredibly sexy.

And I love it when he takes a firm tone with me.

But why would he want a broke college student like me?

Christopher

This wasn't supposed to happen.

Sure, Anna was my type.

Maybe that was why I chose her to be one of the extras in my movie.

But I wasn't ever planning on talking to her.

And then she was injured and I had no choice but to step in.

The more time I spend with Anna, the more I want her.

But she feels indebted to me and that's the last thing I want.

I want to be her Daddy and take care of her.

It only feels natural.

How was I supposed to tell her that without scaring her?

Charismatic Producer Daddy is a short HOT ageplay romance featuring two consenting adults who are perfect for each other. It includes DDLG and ABDL elements, a touch of drama, and a sexy Happily Ever After. Enjoy.

This book is part of a series of standalone stories about Littles and the Daddies that are perfect for them. These books can be read in any order.

Click Here and read ***Charismatic Producer Daddy***!